T.M. Cooks is the pen name of the following collaborative writing team. The contributors are:

- Evie Davidson

- Scarlet Best

- Lauren Hill

- Sandra Korejwo

- Emily Saidi

- Kiana Onyiriuka

- Ella Twadell

- Poppy Phillips

- Melanie Jones

with cover design by Michelle Marham @FelineTrickster (Instagram and Twitter). The project was overseen by Joe Reddington, Dr Yvonne Skipper and Richard Seymour.

The group cheerfully acknowledges the wonderful help given by:

- Matt Barlow

- Mr Herbert

- Tanya Rogers

- Miss Whitehouse

- Kate Hoole

- Andrew Smith

And a big thank you goes to Higher Horizons who funded this wonderful project.

It's been a wonderful opportunity, and everyone involved has been filled with incredible knowledge and enthusiasm.

Finally, we would like to thank all staff at The Oaks Academy for their support in releasing our novelists from lessons for a full week.

The group started to plan out their novel at 9.15 on Monday 28 June 2021 and completed their last proofreading at 13.05 on Friday 2 July 2021.

We are incredibly proud to state that every word of the story, every idea, every chapter and yes, every mistake, is entirely their own work. No teachers, parents or other students touched a single key during this process, and we would ask readers to keep this in mind.

We are sure you will agree that this is an incredible achievement. It has been a true delight and privilege to see this group of young people turn into professional novelists in front of our very eyes.

# The Glitch

**T. M. Cooks**

# Contents

1

# Chapter 1

# The beginning

As Daniel played video games, Ashley stared at him lost in her thoughts, wondering what could be. What if she confessed? What if he rejected her? She had loved him for years, but she was too worried. She didn't think that she could handle getting rejected by him. What if she made a fool of herself? What if he didn't love her back? It couldn't be. She loved him. She had always loved him, but in her mind it was not possible. What if he only sees me as a friend or as a sister? She wanted him to be happy with her. All rational decisions about talking to him had gone out of the window. She trusted him and respected him. All that was in her mind was that she would lose that trust. Lose that respect. Lose their relationship that they have now. In her mind her feelings could never come out. In her mind he could never know under any circumstances. Her true feelings for Daniel was her biggest secret that no one but Ivy knew about. For some reason she trusted Ivy completely; she had no idea why.

Ashley didn't like people. She kept herself to herself. She liked looking and imagining what she could be if she spoke to people. She hated people. Talking to them was her worst nightmare. She had never been one to have a lot of friends; she had always been too scared of what they thought about her. In her mind she had no need to talk to them. If they didn't want to talk to her then she wouldn't talk to them. The only people that Ashley talked to were Daniel and Ivy. They were study partners for English. Even though Ivy had no idea what was going on most of the time. They loved English but they didn't know why. It was because they loved working with each other and each other's company. Ashley could also rely on Ivy for help and advice so she told Ivy about her liking Daniel and Ivy responded,

"You're gonna have to tell him, or I

will."

"I know but I'm not ready yet, " Ashley replied. Would she ever be ready to admit these feelings to him? Probably not. What if he rejected her and it made things awkward for them? What if he would never want to talk to her again? See this is why she won't tell him which is why she will keep this secret until the day she dies. Although some things are better told.

It had its perks being quiet. The amount of gossip she heard. Gossip about forgotten love, lies and hatred. She never told anybody about what she heard, she wrote it down and imagined what she would do if she was in their position. What if she told someone? She could ruin so many people's lives. If she knew this many people she had no idea what she would do. She got upset after a while because she knew she was alone. She knew the consequences of hating people, and she knew the consequences of loving someone; she knew the problems that could be caused. What could happen when you get too attached to people. The heartbreak that would follow. She knew Daniel liked someone but no one could get him to say who it was. Could it be her? A girl can dream. Sometimes dreams can be wishes that we really want to happen. Would this dream become a reality?

The game Daniel was playing was overheating. Sadly they didn't know why or even how to fix it. They also didn't know what this would lead to. It wouldn't be bad would it? May came into the room gleaming with happiness. This was very unusual but they didn't dare ask in fear of losing her smile. It was uncommon for her to be so happy. Nobody had seen her smile for a while. Nobody knew why. There were rumors about something. Something about her past. The rumors were far gone and nobody brings back the past, only the bullies. It was pride that stopped people asking for help if they were down. Pride stopped a lot of things, even happiness. Pride is the one thing that brings people together or apart. The game was buzzing and vibrating. It was like it was a person inside. Daniel shot May a worried look. He always looked to her for support and he wanted it one day to be love. He dropped the controller and backed away. It stopped buzzing and vibrating. It was almost like it was fixed.

"What happened? Can you fix it?" Ivy

asked.

"I hate technology. Why does it never work?"

Daniel slowly shuffled himself towards it. He was worried something might happen to him. He could've never in his wildest dreams guessed what was going to happen next. He had never been superstitious. Even if he saw things he still never believed them. He should start believing what he sees. He gets flashbacks of the past long gone. A past he'd much rather forget. A past with family, hope and joy. A past he didn't ever want to remember. He called May over and they both started to try and fix it.

"No joy, " May sighed. She saw a flash of light. Daniel saw his past. A look of horror filled his face.

11

It stopped and the TV turned black. It looked darker than usual. It almost looked too real. He felt a rising headache. The world began to turn. He saw his past, his family, his friends. He was filled with hope. He was filled with love. A need to sleep, overtook him as his eyes closed without him even knowing. He resisted the sweet temptation of sleep.

He saw May, Ashley, Scarlett, Ivy, all almost glitching. It couldn't be. People don't glitch. Computers glitch. He was confused and tired; he felt drained and exhausted almost as if someone had flipped a switch to make him unnaturally exhausted. All he could think about was sleep and a desert?

# Chapter 2

# The vision of the book

Meanwhile in a world different to reality, the clock in the back was ticking, *tick tock, tick tock.* It was a Victorian clock. The one your grandparents would have and brag about it to the knitting community. The sound of the walnut wood hitting the floor was heard as Nora flipped the pages of her book. She sat in silence taking in the words that were inked onto the pages. Some pages were still white. The book was older then time but still in perfect condition almost like it was newly made. She loved sitting next to her squirrel Monty. Her husband had got him cage after cage, toys after toys. He was only three months old but still very loved. Then she stopped, she stopped reading her book, she stopped rocking back and forth in her wooden chair, then she turned. There was a small nightstand next to her chair, it was the same walnut wood as the chair. Of course with it being Nora it had a doily on. She opened the drawer only to pull out a small doll, a small needle and some fabric pieces. Then the sound of the walnut wood hitting the floor started again. The doll was small and looked like a child that used to visit often with their parents. Nora stroked the doll lovingly like how you would a child's hair. This was one of many dolls, all of the dolls would look strangely familiar to people. Nora then looked into the eyes of the doll.

She felt an uneasy feeling and dropped her sewing, immediately grabbing her book. She felt this way before but that was a long time ago. Flipping through the glitching pages she saw a story. One she hadn't written. Fear struck her heart like a dagger, she had failed to stop people from entering it again. Time was repeating itself and she could do nothing but sit there and watch, as people would have to go through the book pages to reach the end.

If only they were here, then everything could be stopped, but they weren't so the only thing she could do is pray. As she turned the page to see what situation they were in, the five people seemed to be fine, no injuries or anything serious. However they were still in the book which meant that there was a possibility that they still could get out, however she knew she couldn't get them out yet. Nora wanted them to go into the book and explore things, she wanted them to take everything they learned from the book into the outside world. She wanted them to show the world that some people aren't as they seem.

When she flicked the page, a picture began to paint itself, she saw five people trapped inside different rooms. One was a middle aged woman who was in a forest, next was a person with a plant pot on their head in a lake, most strange she thought. Third was a young-adult stranded on a blue beach, fourth was a boy with messy black hair. Then she realised what was happening. Nora was old fashioned, she always wore Victorian clothes that reached the floor. She married at eighteen when she fell pregnant with her first child. Her mother disapproved of her marriage but she married for love and she was willing to risk that. Seventeen children later her love is still blooming, she adores her children. Nobody can remember all their names, there were too many for some to remember, except from her. She married her husband Philip many moons ago. She is now 54. He is now 74. Love was the factor of this family. In Nora's mind love rules all, love

17

can bring people together, create families and create happiness. Love could also create death and depression. In Nora's mind it's up to love. She was a nurse for fifteen years, her main priority is to make the world better no matter what. However, Nora had a side only her husband knows about. A side you will soon know about. She didn't want anyone to see her other side just yet, but she knew she couldn't hide it away forever.

# Chapter 3

# Scarlett wakes up

Scarlett woke up in a tree. Her body ached and hurt. Her eyesight was blurred and fuzzy. She couldn't quite make out shapes or people. She sat up and fell off the branch that was supporting her weight. When her body hit the ground, she let out a grunt of pain and sat up rubbing her temples. Where am I?' She thought. Her surroundings were a dense forest that had thick leaves making it seem darker than it was. The trees were thick and thin all covered in moss. Small mushrooms of all kinds grew from the ground, around the roots of said trees. It all looked oddly familiar to her. She had long black hair with curls. She always wore indie clothes, brightly colored with frills. You never saw her leave the house without makeup. More makeup than a Make up factory. She walked with confidence. She walked with love, love from her mum. Scarlett was loved and happy. She had a girlfriend. Her name was Hannah, that's all they knew about her. Her life was very private and confidential. She told her mum everything about her life. Every Little detail. Love has never been so present, as soon as she woke up all of that was gone.

Scarlett pondered for a bit wondering why there was a pain in her head, she shrugged it off figuring she got drunk and wandered into the forest near to the campus. She stood up, immediately regretting her choice as a wave of dizziness rushed to her brain, almost causing her to topple over.

"God, my girlfriend is going to be so worried about me. I should probably text her to assure I'm alright." She fumbled around in her pockets looking for her cell phone.

"That's strange it isn't here, guess I must have dropped it somewhere. I need to walk around and retrace my steps to find it"'

"Maybe it's this way" she started to

walk south, looking for any items that could be hers, but luck was not on her side.

"Ugh" she groaned, deep in thought, stumbling about the overgrown forest. She was so deep in thought that she didn't see the thick branch in front of her. Scarlett stumbled over said branch and fell onto the leaves below. She picked herself up, her cheeks flushed due to embarrassment.

"Oh my, I hope no one saw that, " she continued walking until she came face to face with a wall. The wall was dirty with blood stained all along the rim, many animals lay around the wall once alive now dead due to starvation. Scarlett was horrified.

Scarlett quickly ran around the edge of the wall, frantically searching for a door or something that could help her escape this reached room. The more she walked the worse the body's appeared. One had half of its body, it's skeletal structure now exposed, with the poor creature's organs hanging out. The smell of all these animals was horrendous, it made Scarlett gag multiple times. When suddenly she spotted something glittering out of the corner of her eye. Immediately she went over to investigate, wanting to leave the stench of death behind.

When Scarlett wandered over to where she saw the glittering, there was something that was most precious to her: the crystals she always kept by her side. She was so worked up when she woke up that she completely forgot about them. She dug around and found the 10 precious crystals, she let out a sigh of relief and held them tightly. She was crying tears of joy

At least everything in this forest wasn't that bad right?

Suddenly through the room all you could hear was the loud mechanical clicking. Scarlett put the crystals in her pocket. The mechanical clicking got louder as the floor started to rumble. She took several steps backwards and the floor where she previously stood began to open. As time went by she saw a wooden door emerging from the depths of the ground. When the door was completely above the ground she took a step towards it and smiled thinking she'll wake up back home and this would just be a terrible dream.

She swung the door open excitedly, a smile starting to etch itself upon her face, but all of a sudden it dropped as she looked inside and was met with a grey room, her eyes welled up with tears as there was nothing in it except from several people, loitering around. Some had terrified expressions, while others were weary and avoiding all others. Scarlett took a step through the door, calmed herself down and tried to say something, but couldn't gain enough confidence after all she had just been through. Once Scarlett was fully through the door it shut behind her creating a loud bang causing several people to weary glance at her then go back to what they were doing. Scarlett went and sat down against the cool wall, worrying about herself and her girlfriend. She cared a lot for her. She cared about her safety and if she was loved enough. They both wanted children. They wanted to raise a family. Hannah wanted

three but Scarlett never brought up the
subject, she was frightened she wouldn't
be a good mother, she was worried she
wouldn't be able to give enough love or affection. She had always had a happy childhood. She wanted her children to have the
same. In her mind yes she killed her dad
but only because she didn't like him. He
was horrible to her and her mum. So he
had to go. She killed him in an accident.
She was casting her spells and he never
woke up. She had been remorseful ever
since. She wanted to try a spell on him
through a book she had read about but he
went up in flames and then burnt to the
ground.

# Chapter 4

# Ivy wakes up

Soggy. Why is it soggy? And cold. The cold is very important because it is cold. Why is there a lake, how is there a lake? When did I get in a cardboard box? Actually this is very comfy. Awwww it's dying. Oooh, a stick, mine. Why is the stick wet? Oh yea, the lake. I should probably get out of it. What's that shiny thing? SHINY!

"Who are you? You look so cool."

"Why thank you, child. My name is Ludociel." The Kraken-like creature responded to the small childlike person.

"Well it's nice to meet you, but I must be going good sir, " Ivy said in an obviously fake posh accent.

"Well, where are you going to go? This seems to be an enclosed space." He responds in an equally silly voice.

"I'm going to collect my son Billy and find a way out. Would you like to join us on our quest?"

"Ahh, there you are, " Ivy says as they pick up Billy, Billy is a pufferfish in a tank with a strap.

"Do you know where anyone else is?" they ask Billy. Billy shakes side to side meaning no.

"Well then we have to find them then!" They cheer.

"Let's go that way!" they shout as they point to the west.

This then starts an adventure that lasts around about three hours. On this journey Ivy collects many items that they find on the ground as well as their pets. This meant that Ivy was ready for anything that would come at them. Ivy had found plants, tape, snacks, a whip, a spork, Hoover and explosives.

"Huh, why is all of this stuff in a forest?" Ivy wondered aloud.

"I do not believe that I have seen these things in the forest before you arrived. Maybe that's because I have never ventured out of the lake."

"OH GOD! Don't scare me like that"

"Apologies young one I didn't mean to give you a fright."

"It's ok just try not to do it in the futureeeee-"

"Child, where are you going?" Ludociel is already used to their behaviour.

"Look at this, doesn't it look cool!" Ivy basically screamed at Ludociel. The book Ivy was holding was an old looking thing, tattered at the edges and a skull intricately carved into the center. The spine looked well worn like it had been used for years, the title was faded and was not legible. The book looked like it was cursed or would curse you.

"I'm gonna open it."

"Young one, I don't think that it will be logical."

"Ok but... I got nothing, I just want

to open it." Before Ludociel could stop them they opened the book. The book was empty except for a page that said something about the lake. It wasn't clear as the book had water damage.

"Hmmmm, I'M GONNA JUMP IN THE LAKE!"

"Why is that what you have gotten from the book?" Ludociel questioned the child-like young adult.

"Mmmmhhh!" Ivy gurgled as they had already dove into the lake.

Suddenly the lake began to bubble, Ludociel began to panic. How could he lose his new companion so quickly? He didn't want to be alone again. In the lake Ivy was blindly searching for something they didn't know about. It could be a person's body for all they know. Then they bashed into something that had a chain on it. So as anyone in Ivy's situation would, they would pull the chain. As the chain was pulled it took a large metal lump with it. This was a plug that was keeping the water in the lake. The lake was like a big sink. The water then began to form a vortex that Ivy was sucked into. On the land next to the lake Ludociel saw the vortex form and sprang in to save Ivy from drowning in it. Once Ivy was pulled from the water Ludociel began to lecture Ivy on why it was highly irresponsible and that they could've drowned. Ivy on the other hand was apologising profusely about making him worry. While being lectured Ivy looked back at the now empty lake,

"Hey, look at that."

"What is so important that you had to

interrupt me?"

"Ummm, I don't know maybe that there's a door at the bottom of the lake."

"WHAT!" Ludociel was shocked that he was sleeping on the exit the whole time.

"Wanna try to open it?"

"I do hope that you aren't planning to do something irresponsible again." Ludociel wasn't sure why he cared about their safety they had only just met, he felt like this random child that he had just found was like his child.

"I can't promise that I won't get hurt but I am gonna jump on it."

"If you are going to do that please try not to get hurt" Ludociel stressed the point of not getting hurt.

"Ok!" Ivy shouted back as they slid down the slope, past remains of skeletons to get to the door. When ivy had reached the bottom they then began to jump. Whilst jumping they were singing songs from kids shows and movies.

"Why is a movie about a group of teenagers being sucked into a game important at this moment in time?" Ludociel questioned the still-jumping person.

"I honestly don't know myself, I just think this one song is really good." By this time Ivy had been jumping for around an hour and a half but didn't lose any energy which confused and amazed Ludociel.

Abruptly, Ivy stopped jumping,

"Ok i'm bored, now is there anything else we can do?"

"My child, there is nothing else to do except try to get out." This answer disappointed they but they understood. Ivy began to search their pockets to find something that could make their job a lot easier. They were also talking to Ludociel about family. Through this, Ivy learnt that Ludociel had no family and that he was the last of his kind, so Ivy invited him to be a part of their family of animals. Ivy explained that they have two mums and that one is the goddess of nature while their other is the goddess of water. Ivy had to then explain that they were made from a glitch in a code and that their mothers raised them, but their mums sent them away to a safer place, away from all of the chaos. This discussion was happening while Ivy was looking for one thing in particular, something they had picked up earlier on the shoreline of the lake.

That thing was the explosives. If they

couldn't break it open by jumping, then they would blow it up.

"Child, what are you going to do with that? Don't hurt yourself."

"I won't or at least i'll try, " with this Ivy began to make a small pile of the explosives.

"Now how do you set these off?" Ivy questioned aloud.

"So you're telling me you have all of this stuff but you have no clue how to use it?" Ludociel asked in disbelief.

"Well I thought that you would've known. Do you not know?" Ivy really had thought that Ludoceil would've known.

"Maybe the book would know?"

"I don't think that the book is a very safe option, but it seems to be the only option we have." With that confirmation

Ivy began to flick through the book. Then after almost giving up hope, there was a page that had the exact instructions you needed to set off the explosives.

"Well, that's certainly strange but so cool!" This seriously concerned Ludociel as this page wasn't there when they checked before. Ivy then began to prepare the explosives for detonation. Once they were prepared Ivy ran from the pile when they were a safe distance from it, it was set off. When the smoke had risen the hole which once held the door was exposed. They both cheered in delight when they realised they could get out. All of them ran through, scared that it may close before they could get out. Once they got out of the room they saw some people. Who were they? Were they in the same situation?

"Ohhhh is that a spork?"

# Chapter 5

# Ashley wakes up

After the game randomly broke, Ashley suddenly appeared at a beach in the middle of nowhere. The beach was so colourful. The sand was the purest white, the ocean was the brightest blue and the trees were as tall as skyscrapers. It was the best thing she had ever seen in her life. The thought of why she was there had

completely left her mind as she was mes-
merised by her surroundings. All of her
worries left her for a while and she completely forgot about all things important
and was just focused on this magical place.
It was the most perfect place and she had
always wanted to go somewhere like this.
It was so perfect it was almost as if someone read her mind and made it reality,
maybe she had a dream and someone was
watching her. It was beautiful and relax-
ing until she realised she was all alone with
no memory of how she got here and no one
to help her out so she decided, she should
probably find a way out of here or at least
something to help her leave this place.

Did someone bring her here? She decided she should go home not for herself
but for her mother. She couldn't stay here

no matter how much she wanted to. No matter how much she wanted to stay, she couldn't. She had always wanted to go somewhere like this. Would it be that bad if she stayed here just for a while? No she couldn't, she had to leave. But she had absolutely no clue where to go. This place wasn't familiar at all, she had never seen anywhere like this. She tried to dive into her memory, to figure out if she had ever been here but there was absolutely nothing.

Ashley quickly decided the best thing to do was explore and see if she could find something to help her out of here. She had remembered something her father had taught her when they went on a family holiday

"If you're ever lost, follow the stars at

night and they'll guide you to where you need to go." She was very close to her father even though he was always at work, she was quite fond of him and how much he did for and her mother. Ashley was very grateful for what he did and wished she could help her mother as much as he did. Her mother was very ill, however she insisted on always helping around the house or trying to get a job to help out even though she was not allowed to, and she knew that. Ashley had always felt bad for her mother and the way she had to live, but Ashley knew that it was the only way to help her and make her get better even though it had never worked. That's why Ashley thought it was pointless and her mother knew that too; She had always thought that they should let her mother do her own things so it would take her mind off her illness, but she would never want to make her mother or father angry so she kept these thoughts to herself.

Ashley realised that if she got here there must be a way to get back out. Ashley wasn't against being alone; she had just gotten so used to Daniel always being around that if there was any time it was quiet she found it annoying and unfamiliar. She thought that when it's quiet it gives her too much thinking time which would lead to her overthinking or becoming too involved in something. Most of the time she would leave important things to Daniel as he would take control and help her out but most of the time it would end in her doing it anyway. She often found herself thinking about Daniel a lot more than she probably should and thinking about what her life would be like if she would just tell him she liked him. But, of course she's never going to tell him unless it was a life or death situation and even then she would be petrified to tell him and ruin what they had together. They have always been really close so she didn't know what she would do without him and his trust. Being apart from Daniel, made her realise how much she actually cared for him and how much she needed him. Whether he knew it or not she needed him and she hoped he would need her too. She hoped that he felt the same way as she did.

After Ashley had explored this tropical paradise for a while she found some sort of challenge which she thought she must have to complete to escape, but no matter how much she wanted to stay here. Luckily for Ashley the challenge was like a code that she had to decipher to unlock some sort of box. She liked puzzles and codes. They reminded her of her childhood when her family would come over and they would do puzzles and they would try and trick her but she would never fall for it. Once she had figured out the code which only took her a few minutes she decided to double check the code to make sure nothing could go wrong as she didn't know what would happen if she made a mistake. Once she finished the final details of the code a mysterious latch opened revealing a door which she guessed was her way out of this surreal place. She walked through the door and was met with a bland coloured room, filled with a large group of people that she had never met before. She took in her surroundings and noticed that several more doors were open, one leading to the bottom of a lake. She sat down next to the doorframe and waited for anyone she could would to appear.

# Chapter 6

# Daniel wakes up

Daniel's eyes opened slowly, only to see a blue sky. He wanted to know where he was. What had happened to him. He moved his hand only to feel a grainy substance, he dug his hand into the substance and grabbed a handful. His head felt like it was on a spike. He looked around, he wanted to know where he was. He sat up and held the odd grainy thing in his hand, it slipped out as his hand got looser. It looks too realistic. Too sandy, too normal. Was It sand? How did I get here? Then he heard it, the laughs of the people he loved the most. Laughter of happiness. He instantly felt warm and loved. How? How were they here? Was it his family? It couldn't be. They died when he was ten. He saw it happen while he was there. His heart felt lighter, his head felt he was flying. Flying with happiness Daniel was loved again. He flung himself up almost immediately, and there right in front of him were his parents and Ashley, the emotions he felt nearly brought him to tears. He went to stand up to run over to them, until he felt something else. It replaced the emotions of sheer joy. It was like a comforting feeling but it was a feeling of fear at the same time. As he tried to figure out the emotions he was feeling he saw everyone start to walk away. He tried to scream but it didn't work. He dropped to his knees as he watched the people he cared for the most walk away and never look back. It was then he heard something, a deep unfamiliar voice.

"Find the key, " The Deep voice said, Daniel sat there. He didn't know what to do.

"Find the key, " It repeated.

"What..? What if I don't"

"You die on the spot" Daniel thought for a minute, the voice might be lying. Daniel had no reason to trust the voice, it could be lying to him. Daniel eventually decided that it would be a good idea to heed the voice's warning.

"How am I meant to find a key in a desert?" It was then that Daniel's feet started walking for him. His hand reached out and then he felt a cold metal, as he picked up a key.

"A key?"

"Danny" a voice squeaked out, it was Ashley's voice. Daniel grinned to himself, he loved it when Ashley called him that. He was still so confused though, he didn't have a clue where he was. Obviously he was in a desert but he had never been to a desert. He stood for a minute to try and figure out where to go next. He had a key but if he used the key on the door would he come out alive, that's what he was more concerned about, he still had so much to do, like get his first job and confess to Ashley. The key was golden and heavy like iron. One day he would confess to her, then they would have a beautiful wedding. A white wedding to the love of his life. A wedding everyone would remember. He had dreamed about that moment since the moment he saw her four years ago. His dreams were all that kept him going. Kept him hoping, they kept him believing. His parents wouldn't be there to see it though. That was probably the worst thing to think about at that moment. He really missed them, it was probably not the best to show him his parents. The more he thinks about them, the worse he feels. That didn't matter though, he needed to figure out how to get out of this place. He didn't want to be left behind, he put the key in the door, turned it and braced himself; he had no clue what was going to be behind the door. It could be a trap, it could honestly be anything. He opened the door and stood for a minute. It was a hallway crammed with pictures. Maybe somebody needed saving. He could be the stereotypical hero. A hero everyone expected him to be. He could save a woman from the big bad wolf. He could be famous. Everyone likes a hero. He arrived at the end of the hallway but there was nothing but a bleek grey room.

# Chapter 7

# May wakes up

As she opened her tired eyes, she was welcomed to a derelict site of some sort; hindered by what seemed like an army of vermin, it held an overwhelming sense of insecurity and vulnerability, but for some strange reason, she related to it. Though broken on the outside, the inside leads to a surge of adventure and undisclosed secrets.

The secrets of May Black.

Running her fingers through the blood stained ancient walls, it lured her in it's dark wonders. Why was she here? She tried her best to think of any slight relation, but nothing came to mind. All that could be done was to stand mesmerized at the withered wood arches, and broken crystal chandeliers engrossed in layers of dust. Then she wondered, what was beyond that room? Maybe, an ancient realm of the gods, or the former residence of a Baroness - one's imagination can never be too great.

As she descended down the stairs she was accompanied by a trail of rhythmic creaks - that's when she heard it - a scream. She clutched the banister in an urge of safety and looked around her tentatively.

What was going on? Was this a figment of her imagination? Running down the stairs as quickly as possible, she locked herself in the nearest room not caring to check it first, as it would probably be less problematic.

It all began at the party. A kind girl named Ashley invited May to it and to be honest, she really didn't want to go. However she went anyway as she didn't want to make a bad impression, so she stayed silent and minded her own business as she always did. However, some imbecile named Daniel decided that it would be a good idea to make her help him fix the TV that had broken, did she look like a technical electrician to him? Even so, she still decided to help, as she would be more invisible. Maybe she should've said 'No' but she was sure that wouldn't get him to leave. So she helped, that probably was the worst decision she made. If she had been quiet or said 'No' she wouldn't be in this situation, but oh well.

She sat crouched in the dusty corner of what looked like an isolated room, with the exception of the long dead corpse that sat in the corner opposite to her. However she didn't realize this and continued to feel alone but, why did she feel so alone? She was used to it, however this somehow felt completely different, but this house somewhat felt familiar. Like something she had put away long ago. A great sense of anger took over her as this place seemed to obtain secrets that she wished to erase, secrets she wished she didn't have to keep. May hugged her knees and tried to block out the thoughts that tried to enter her mind wanting to be left alone. But to no avail they entered her mind as she found herself looking back on the things she tried so desperately to erase but it just wouldn't work.

Having never had a parental figure to guide her through the wrongs and rights in her life, she was ever so grateful for it. In her eyes, parents were obstacles - they got in your way and prevented you from progressing any further all because they obtained a 'vision' for you. Most of the time they were unsure of what that 'vision' really was. Her parents abandoned her at the age of 5 years old as they couldn't afford to look after her because of their 'current affairs' - aka drugs. She was then taken into care and her life had gone downhill ever since. She'd always held an infinite grudge against them, one so passionate she speculated whether she'd ever come to terms with it. Parents were supposed to guide you, show you what life is and teach you things nobody else can teach you. But they didn't do that, they didn't stay to teach her how to ride a bike or how to tie her shoelace. They just left her all alone with nothing. This is probably why she almost didn't have feelings anymore; she just got on with life and kept to herself.

Staring into space, she wondered how the others were getting on; did they suspect that she's the mole? A mole is described as something or someone undercover that is working for a particular agency, to obtain vital information. This role was paramount for May as this experiment was a way that she could see how the average person would react to challenging situations - it was a way to see what was 'normal'. As a young girl, she was viciously bullied for the way she was, as she wasn't perceived as beautiful or pretty, just a freak made from the wrath of the devil. She didn't mind that people had such negative perceptions of her as who were they to say these things about her? To her they were just lesser beings who had no sense of purpose. If they knew the real May they would probably be more accepting and not as judgy towards her. It's just that May wasn't considered as their type of person but if they actually got to know her they would probably use her to gain more of a social status.

After a while of cradling in the mind's

obscurity, she decided that she wanted to venture outside this claustrophobic room. In the corner of her eye she noticed a somewhat vague shadow below the arched door frame with a pattern that cascaded into the floor. At first she had the courage to ignore such a thing, but then it whispered her name in a hoarse cry,

"May, come here!"

It was persistent but getting impatient,

"MAY, COME HERE AND SEE WHAT YOU DID!"

With that, it disappeared into the deep depth of the abandoned dwelling. She turned and smiled whispering under her breath,

"Well, you deserved it." She halted as the form of a deep mahogany door appeared; she reluctantly opened it and entered into a whirl of darkness. It was time.

# Chapter 8

# The game starts

"So where are we?" May asked. Everyone looked at her, some scared and some
confused.

"Well the last I remember I was at a
party." Daniel remembered. The room
was grey with a doorway ahead. The floor,
ceiling and walls were all covered in metal
plates. While everyone else was trying to

figure out what to do and where to go, a group of girls stood in the corner of the room, deep in conversation. Ivy stood for a second, thinking about the situation in front of them. How suspicious, the people in this room have probably never really had a whole conversation so why do these people seem so chatty? Maybe they were trying to get answers? Who knows?

One of the girls spoke up. They were a tall figure, with bright pink hair that went down to her thighs. She was dressed in a black long sleeved jumper, with a white corset. Her dark blue skirt perfectly contrasted the white. Her legs were covered with tall thigh high socks and on the right leg were bandages.

"So.. we all don't know where we are or how we got here so let's start with an introduction" the pink haired girl suggested, with a soft tone. Murmurs of agreement were heard throughout the room.

"Well anyways, let me start, " the girl said energetically.

"My name's Elextha pronounced Elexthia, I'm 22 years old and I'm a 6'2 and I'm a male."

"Male?!" a boy with black hair exclaimed.

"Yes a male, I thought that was obvious?" Elextha answered. A dirty brown haired person bluntly said,

"Is your name pronounced Elex-ha or Ele-xtha?" Elextha's face fell

"NO!... sorry I get annoyed when people say my name wrong, but most people don't understand my name anyways so just call me Lex!" the dirty brown haired person spoke next,

65

"Hey, hey! My name is Ivy! Isn't that right Billy!" the pufferfish they were carrying in the bucket nodded up and down.

"I'm 19! And please refer to me with they/them!" After Ivy finished shouting out their introduction, an older looking person asked a question,

"Why do you have a plant pot on your head?"

"Ehh? I have a plant pot on my head?" Elextha turned around, He stood staring at a girl for a moment before speaking up.

"It's your turn, " The girl with messy brown hair looked up at the man for a second, and then after letting out a huge sigh, spoke.

"The name is Pix, "

"Haha, come on Pix, you need to say a little more than that"

"I'm 21."

"That will do, " Elextha replied.

All their minds were racing. Their heart was beating fast.Their blood was pounding. She felt unsteady on her feet. They were all concerned. Ashley looked around the room. She was studying every object. Her eyesight was not the best so she studied every object with her hand. She felt the velvet sand run through her fingers. She wanted to go home. She wanted to be with Daniel. As soon as she thought about him he lay a hand on her shoulder to comfort her. It comforted her knowing she had someone she trusted close by. May shot them both a glare. She couldn't read May. May was too complex. You never knew where you stood with her. Ashley thought a part of her was jealous. Jealous of the trust they both had with each other. The one question she always asked herself, was what if.

A deep grumble shook the ground as the room began to get considerably smaller.

"What's going on?" screamed Ashley.

"I don't know, but don't worry, I'll keep you safe!" Daniel reassured Ashley whilst looking her deeply in her eyes. This was followed by an intense 10 seconds of eye contact.

"Will you two 'lovebirds' stop' your little love fest and focus on how were going to get out?" said May with a tone as dead as her soul.

"There's a key near the door but it's locked in a box, " said Scarlett. "It also needs another key!"

"Great! How are we going to get out

then, there must be some type of coding that we can interpret to find the other key right?" Asked Pix

"Well, it's not that simple, " stated Elextha. "You can't just find a code, you have to look at what's around you and figure out what it links to, at least that's what I think."

The group then looked for anything that stood out to them, or anything that didn't look right. If they were to figure out what this was, they could use it by deciphering it and creating a key.

As they thoroughly searched the room, they noticed a peculiar object in the corner of the room. A small odd shaped phenomenon that lacked poise and character, seeming to be there on purpose. Intrigued by it's fascinating nature, Ivy grabbed it in excitement.

"What's this?" asked Ivy.

"What's what?" replied Daniel with a carved expression of compulsion.

"This thing!" Ivy exclaimed.

"Wait, that might be the clue we can decipher!" said Scarlett with a tone of excitement.

"Hold your horses love, we need to outgo a prominent examination of it first, because it could be a trap." Intruded Pix with a tinge of sass and sarcasm.

As they examined the outlandish object it seemed to fit the needed description. They deciphered the code it held and it formed into a key. A sense of relief filled the room as they were one step closer to getting out.

A simple twist and turn and the box

was open. Gracefully the key fell into the hands of Scarlett, in a matter of seconds she opened the next door and another adventure was to be explored.

# Chapter 9

# The Alert

Dr Spencer's anger got the best of him and the two things that calmed him down was playing sports and coding. One of those was out of the picture as it has been pouring it down for two weeks straight. So what did he do, he started to code. The game he made was only for him to play on his PC whenever he was bored, yet people had access to it all over the world.

The typical day for Spencer is not typical to many people, as he is a nineteen year old professor. The first thing he does is workout and plays a sport at five-thirty in the morning as he wanted to be an athlete but never made it. Then he gets dressed for work which he hates as he loves to wear streetwear and hats, however he makes it work. Then when his lessons are over he meets his friends who turn out to be his students, for a couple of hours. After hanging out he has another job which is a programmer. He only does this three times a week. On this particular day he did not have to do his extra job.

Spencer was watching the newest movie at the time with his friends after class and he got an alert which created a flood of frustration.

"Shush!"

His friends wondered what it was.

"What was that, is it important?" and Spencer replied,

"Nothing, it's fine we should finish watching this before I check on it."

They ended up finishing the film, after that they all got food at the closest place possible and went shopping for some brand new shoes. Once they finished, they forgot all about the alert until he got back.

Spencer James' house had a spare room for a couple of years and he decided to make it a home office. It was very much like Dr Spencer James. The walls had computer circuit print wallpaper and on one wall there was a load of trainers he had collected in transparent boxes. His house was in a back alley. As soon as you looked out of the window you would see things nobody should see. For example rubbish. It fueled him into working hard so he could get out of the place. His dream place was a London modern home fit for a family to be raised in. All of his siblings argued who got the room, but Spencer is the youngest, so of course he got it. His siblings slightly hated him for this. They knew it wasn't his fault but there was still this, what if in his mind.

When he had finished in the cinema, he headed straight to his office to check on his code. He stared at it in complete confusion, it was messed up again. Dr Spencer James had been trying to fix the game for a long time, but for some odd reason, it kept glitching and messing up.

"God dammit" he said while hitting the table in anger.

His efforts to fix the game were going terribly. He couldn't figure out what was going on. With his hands on the table, he leaned in closer to the screen, searching for an idea on how to fix the stupid thing. He knew if he couldn't fix the coding, the game progress wouldn't move forward. If the game wouldn't move forward, then it would fail completely and shut down forever. He obviously didn't want that, he worked so unbelievably hard on this game.The coding, everything. It was his pride and joy at this point. Not only that, this game was released to the public and they absolutely loved it. What would happen if he took it away?

# Chapter 10

# The First Dilemma

They came to a dead end or at least they thought it was a dead end, until a door showed up beckoning them into the room. Where did it come from? It was as if they had to head towards that direction, because it was the only way. When they went through the door and was shown that gave them two options to choose from. It didn't seem hard to choose, right? To make things more difficult and pressurising, a timer was added. The timer was soon forgotten about. No one knew what was happening, or how this came about. To get out, they had to go forward. They all wished that they didn't have to continue on but to get out was the only way.

As they made their way further they reached a split off point. A surge of confusion rose. How was this possible? Who was doing this? Who would do such a thing? Everyone was wondering who was behind this. Then out of nowhere a screen emerged from the ceiling. On this screen two options appeared, one was to save a child from dying, the other offered money-a life changing amount. This seemed to be easy. But not everything is as easy as it looks. Most immediately everyone moved down the corridor to save the child, only Elextha stayed. Everyone was shocked that he stayed. Was he actually going to let a child die just for some money?

It was time, time for Elextha to choose. A choice between saving a child or obtaining a lot of money. They all thought that saving the child was the obvious option, however Elextha had a different idea. He chose the money.

"Money! Money is what I want, just think of all the things I could do with it!" he screamed with joy.

.

Everyone looked at Elextha like he was crazy, his smile grew wider turning into a menacing grin. "What can I say, money's just more of my thing. Who even cares about saving one life anyways-" his sentence was cut short. Everyone turned to the timer that had been forgotten for so long.

It had made itself known by emitting an annoying sound. *Beep, beep, beep.* Everyone covered their ears. The noise felt like it was piercing their skulls. After the beeping, there was a sound of a mechanical clicking. When suddenly two dozen thin spears impaled Elextha. His body was lifted up with the pure force and speed of the spears. Everyone stared. They were frozen and unable to do anything. His menacing facial expression immediately dropped into a look of pure fear. Blood ran out of his mouth like a waterfall, his hands also covered in the thick liquid.

"Th-this wasn-n't supp-pposed t-to happen-n-..." tears began to fall from his eyes, through his eyes you could see the pain and sorrow. *How could this happen?*

"Gu-gu-ess th-his, " he paused, coughing up more blood *Why did this happen?*

"I-it I-is wha-t I-I de-eserv-ve.. ri-gght?" was all he said before his body went limp. The spikes retracted slowly and painfully, leaving his body on the ground. His blood now splattered all over the walls and floor. He was no more. Sorrow filled the room. No one could believe that something like that could happen in front of them.

Out of nowhere, the floor tore open revealing a furnace. His body was then dropped into a furnace like bag of coal. Undignified, unloved, and not wanted. Nobody expected this. Nobody wanted this. Life was not present, but death was. Death can control people like a child with a doll, unable to move and can only talk and walk on demand of the human. The smell of the corpse was not yet present and the devil was still unaware of what was to come. Sorrow loomed over everyone like a dark cloud - not everyone will grieve, but they will all feel. Then there was a flash. A flash of light, a flash of evil. Death suffocated them like a blanket, little did they know who was watching. Watching their every move, their every breath. The smell of burning flesh began to invade the room.

Grieving, they left the room. Still shaken and confused. Ashley stared at Daniel looking for comfort. Daniel turned away from his friends, this was too close to home for him. Comfort was not enough, he didn't want to relive this, not now, not ever. A person who comprehends loss should never experience that pain again. As loss destroys families, loss destroys lives, loss tears the heart out of everyone who knew them. It never leaves once it's present. For Daniel his heart was already broken. It was now shattered, shattered into little pieces. The King of Hell had won, Lucifer was the winner of death and the winner of hate filled with temptation. If Dr Spencer was present he would say that desire is the mark of the devil. He was a Christian and in these times, it gives people hope, faith makes you stronger. Elextha grew weak and gave into these desires. Would anyone else?

# Chapter 11

# Trying to fix the problem

Soon after Dr Spencer James found the error in his code, he thought that he messed it up himself whilst making the game and only just noticed. That it was a common mistake that could be easily fixed, everyone makes mistakes from time to time.

However there was something unusual: the code was like nothing he had seen before and he studied almost every coding language. This had shocked him. How could this have happened? Since he had written the whole code it made him do some research into this new coding language he had just discovered. He found out it was one of the only ones he didn't study. He couldn't believe that the code had appeared. He began to question when it was added, why was it there. He began to investigate where it had come from.

Spencer James had always been smart, most would call him a child genius. His sister was the first person to ever notice. He was three at the time and she was fourteen Spencer was writing on a whiteboard and he did math equations made for sixteen year olds. As he got older he got smarter, when he was a mere fifteen years old he graduated from University and got his PhD at the age of seventeen. Dr Spencer James got his PhD in computer science and taught at the Uni for two years. It kind of ruined his social life being so smart, so he never made many friends as he didn't stay in a single school for long enough, however he has had two best friends from primary school who didn't mind that he wouldn't stay at their school for long. His best friends Jaxon and Levi just started Uni whilst their best friend was teaching there. This made some of their interactions a bit strange.

Dr Spencer James had a difficult time as a child his parents never really got along that well and he was the youngest of five.

He had three brothers and one sister. He always went to his siblings for help instead of his parents as he always felt like a burden as his parents were always fighting. This would have a long term effect on how he sees love and relationships. At the age of nine, his parents split which was the best decision for his whole family. For six months after the divorce he saw his mother on the weekends, then one day everything changed when she disappeared and he never heard from her again. From the day she left he developed anger towards his mother and took it out on anything and anyone he could. This made him hold a strong dislike and a border line hatred towards anyone who looked like his mom. It didn't help that they moved to the UK from New York when his mom left at a young age. As this put Spencer in an extremely stressful situation. Moving across the world is hard enough but just after losing a parent it would be even harder for any one.

With all of his anger he needed an outlet. Many people use their hobbies to try to calm them down and put their anger somewhere else. Some would do sport or paint and either paint or play out their feelings. For Dr James he loves to code and it calms him, but people at his school did not agree and they said that if he were to fit in he would need a better hobby like basketball or football. This led the school to collectively outcast him. All of the stress caused Spencer to drop out of school and he worked on a game no one would see. This game was his pride and joy, not like anyone would see it though.

However his older brother thought it was too good to go to waste so he got Spencer to release a beta copy. Once the public saw the game they were hooked. Spencer updated it every month, after the shock of it being used by the public. If there was anyone doing anything he didn't like, he would change the rules so overtime the rules had completely changed. This would cause some problems in the future. Not that anyone would figure out any time soon.

# Chapter 12

# Suspicions

May seemed to be moving everyone away in the opposite direction of where they wanted to go. This made Ivy suspicious. Why would you do that unless you had something to hide? May seemed to intimidate them.

"No guys come on, there's probably nothing here, let's go somewhere else." May said coldly, everyone nods as they're scared of her, especially when she's angry. Ivy follows as well but is more suspicious.

Ivy watched May as she acted very on edge and not much like herself. She was very tense and she's trying to go behind everyone to keep anyone from looking back. What was behind them? Was it something bad? Ivy trusts themself, Ludociel also believed that May was the mole. How could Ivy get anyone to believe them? They looked around for people they trust and realise they are close to Scarlett, their University Professor would believe them right?

They decided to make themselves known to Scarlett. They come up to her as everyone walked ahead Scarlett and Ivy walk at their own pace as Scarlett looks at them confused

Ivy decides to try to talk to Scarlett.Scarlett notices this and asks "What do you need Ivy?"

"I have a bad feeling about May." Ivy states while staring dead at May "Ok then tell me while we walk ok?" Scarlett nods

Ivy starts explaining their reasons for being suspicious of May. Scarlett looks at them in disbelief as Ivy abruptly stops talking, they started staring at Scarlett

"What's wrong?". Scarlett questioned and laughs softly. Ivy doesn't speak, just stared into the distance,

"Whatever kiddo you really don't understand games.." Scarlett catches up to everyone leaving Ivy. Ivy sighed,

"Why can't they see something is wrong? Why don't they believe us, Ludociel?" Scarlett shrugs it off not believing Ivy because she's been here before and doesn't believe anything is wrong with how it is going. She was wrong. She would regret thinking that.

"That child is a bit odd, " She thought aloud, as she rejoined everyone. She shook her head to try and get the doubts out of it.

"Whatever" As Scarlet continued to walk, Ivy tried to catch up to speak to her. Scarlett doesn't notice and tries to ignore anyone who speaks to her while she collects her thoughts.

"Please just believe me, come on, " At this point Ivy was getting annoyed that no one believed them.

"Even Ludociel feels like there is something wrong." Scarlett ignored them.

"Scarlett, why can't you just see the

bigger picture right now." Scarlett sighed, getting slightly annoyed by the constant talking.

"Why don't you believe me, can't you see I'm trying to help?" Scarlett kept ignoring Ivy. Everyone was confused at why Scarlett was annoyed and Ivy began to get angry.

Scarlett continued to ignore them. Then Scarlett shouted,

"NO! Just shut up, I don't care." Anger was over taking her. This made Ivy go quiet as they didn't realise that they were annoying Scarlett. Scarlett walked off again, annoyed at Ivy. Ivy sighs and just slowly walks behind everyone sadly while trying to think of what to do. Ivy says to themselves

"Now who will believe me?"

"My child, I believe you. Have you thought about checking that book you picked up?" Although Ludociel didn't trust the book at all, he needed to believe that it could help them.

"Ohh, I forgot about that."

"How?"

# Chapter 13

# The Meeting

Spencer overheard Nora talking on the phone.

"I swear my book is REAL! I have to go, someone is knocking on the door. Don't think I will forget about this!"

"Hello, I couldn't help but overhear your conversation. What book is it?" Spencer asked politely, curious of what he had heard.

"I have my own book that I have written, and I can see visions of people playing a game about it."

"Did you just say a game?" Spencer looked confused. How could she know?

"Yes, why?" Nora narrowed her eyes. Her eyesight was not the greatest at the best of times, and in a small lab room it was even worse.

"I have a lot of explaining to do. I think it best if you come in."

"Yes, of course."

"I'm all ears" says Nora.

Spencer tells Nora how he created a game, and when he overheard Nora talk about the book, he had to find out if his game and her book had any relation.

"Here's the book."

Spencer had a flick through some pages and read some of it - it was exactly the same.

"I can transport in and out of the game by reading it, so I'm afraid I will not be able to show you certain pages; it has also come to my attention that the future is unclear for these people."

Nora suddenly felt unwell. She was worried about the people trapped there, but she put her feelings to one side. She was a closed book with a lock nobody had a key to.

Nora felt as if she could trust Spencer now and she eventually revealed that there are real people stuck in a game he computerised from a board game he used to play ( which was connected to her book). Eventually she told him all there is to know. Every last thing. At least everything she knew but there's probably a lot of things she didn't know about

Nora had the book in her possession at first, but somehow, it must have got into someone else's custody for a short amount of time. It had also been converted into a board game - which is where Spencer got his inspiration for his video game from. Nora eventually confides in Spencer that - "The book that I have is the inspiration for the game you used for your video game."

Spencer replied in a shocked and shaky voice.

"S-so I made a game that involves some sort of magic."

"Yes!" Nora exclaimed in frustration.

Spencer was in utter disbelief.

"I don't believe you! It can't be." Nora grew more concerned that he didn't believe her as maybe he would do something terrible to the game that could end lives or even worse - humanity.

Spencer stood up with his head in his hand,

"I need to think about this; it's kinda a lot to take in."

"For heaven and hell use formal English. It can't be a large shock can it?" She began to grow angry with the lack of communication with her. She was also petrified he wouldn't believe her.

"Please leave, I am very busy and don't have time for boys who don't speak about their feelings, or indeed communicate with anybody."

"I'm not a boy, I'm a man! You've just given me information that's extremely hard to digest, so if anyones acting like a child it's YOU!"

He shuffled away still gathering his thoughts. Nora began to weep; she had not cried like that in as long as she could remember. Nobody could make her cry, not even the devil Lucifer himself. All she wanted was comfort and help. She grew lonely even having borne seventeen children. She had always said that, 'loneliness can come with even a room full of people'. She sobbed until she could sob no more. Then out of nowhere, there was a bang. She stopped and stood up expecting someone. Was her reputation of cold morraled Nora gone? She went to check the stock room, but it was just a window shutting - A great sense of relief washed over her. She might look cold but in truth she was kind and loving.

She knew everyone as she delivered them

all. She had seen the mothers cry in pain as she delivered a life into the world. It was a small town where everyone knew each other's business and secrets. She liked it like that. She liked the closeness and the love everyone had for each other. They all came to her for support. Many years ago, she left her mother for the love of her husband Philip, she had no family except the children. The children she loved dearly. As the days went by, she grew warmer thinking about her children. Even when parents needed a rest they came to her as they knew she'd do the job thoroughly. Deep down she knew it was actually because the kids liked her and looked up to her even if, sometimes they were scared of her. It might be sugary sweet but it was a community, a community all under her

power. The power she had and no matter how hard they tried, all that happened
was the power grew stronger.

# Chapter 14

# The choice

"Your second task is for Daniel. Daniel has to choose between saving Ashley who is drowning or save the group from a fire. Your time will start now, good luck." He looks at the timer nervously to see how long he has left. He knew what decision he made impacted his whole life. He looks around as if someone is going to help him and sees that no one was going to help him and he makes his way to the door with his friends in it. However something prevents him from going to open the door and he felt a pull that made him change direction and walk towards the door with Ashley in. He didn't want to go to Ashley because then people would find out his true feelings for her but no matter how hard Daniel tried he couldn't move away from Ashley. It was like something was living inside him and controlling him. After a while he let go and followed his feet. He walked through the door to save Ashley and heard a voice say

"You would choose a girl over all your friends." This made Daniel tear up but he knew the game was just messing with his head. He ran through the door, tears streamed down his face with regret and he was scared to face his friends because they would know what door he went through and what was in it. As soon as he got to the end he felt a sharp pain in his chest and he fell through the door.

On the other side of the door was Ashley and all his friends. Daniel fell to the floor twisting and turning, bones creaking and breaking due to the immense contortion that he was undergoing. Everyone could tell he was in pain. That's when they saw the devil look through Daniel's now bleeding eyes. May called a silent meeting and everyone went over to the side away from Daniel so the devil inside would not hear them speaking. Ashley stayed with Daniel and tried to calm him down, and stop him bleeding so that he would not die. May said that this specific devil Daniel is possessed by is called Lucifer and that the only way to get Lucifer out of Daniel is for Daniel to remember why he is still living.

"Ashley can make Daniel remember, " Ivy said.

"Why me??" Ashley replied.

"You and I know why!" Ashley looked over to where Daniel was, he now had several bones poking out of him and a pool of blood was forming underneath him. His eyes were completely blood stained and blood started to leak out from his mouth. Ashley spoke in a kind soft tone.

"Ok. Daniel, why are you still living??" Daniel answered, causing more blood to pour from his mouth.

"F-for. M-my..mu-um....an-n..dd-ad-!!"

"Keep going, " May whispered.

"Uhh anything else Danny?" Ashley asked.

"I love it when you call me Danny." Daniel's face pulled up to a shaky smile. Black smoke came poured out of Daniel's eyes and mouth, like a cloud evaporating water. No one had ever seen a devil before. He had crimson red eyes. The only words he said before disappearing were "Well done Ashley." His bloodshot eyes turned back to normal, and his body started to heal. Ashley was thankful to see that she had actually saved Daniel's life.

She hugs Daniel tightly, happy to see him alive and he hugs back softly, whispering to her smiling

"Thank you Ashley." Ashley helps him stand up slowly holding him as Ivy helps and they all try to catch up to the others.

"It's alright Daniel. I guess we are even now seeing as you went through the door to save me."

"Oh you saw that! Well, you're my best friend so that's why I went through that door!" Daniel gave Ashley a nervous smile. She smiled but she couldn't help feeling a bit heartbroken.

# Chapter 15

# Discovery

"The coding is messed up again, " said a confused Dr Spencer James, staring at the screen as he watched the coding glitch from his improved version to the old version. With a frustrated sigh he sat down on his black leather chair. He sat thinking for a moment what he could do. He turned to his wall to try and get some type idea, when he noticed something. It was the book that inspired the whole game idea. He threw himself off his chair and practically ran out of the university. After bumping into multiple students he finally arrived at his destination.

Nora's head turned toward the door as she watched her fellow colleague pant.

"Can I help you Spencer?" the woman's head tilted in surprise.

"I need to talk to you, " a still panting Spencer said through deep breaths.

"May I suggest Coffee?" Nora gave a warm smile as she walked by.

After some stairs and a long silence the red Costa sign came into view, as Spencer walked towards it. Nora stopped.

"Wow Spencer, I didn't make you out to be such a felon." She turned around and gave Spencer a look of pure disgust. If looks could kill Spencer would definitely be dead by now.

"We are not going into such a filthy establishment, we are going to that one over there."

Nora pointed to a much smaller cafe with flowers around the door. Spencer stood there for a second in absolute shock and disbelief, but once he regained his senses he started following Nora again. Nora continued to the counter where she ordered a Earl Grey tea, Spencer being a man who was not as fancy just ordered a simple iced tea.

"So Spencer, what is it that you would like to so eagerly talk to me about?" The woman took a sip of the scorching tea.

"Well I thought about the book you

were telling me about and well I think it has something to do with the game I'm creating." The man fiddled with his fingers, hoping she didn't think he was crazy.

"Ah yes that makes sense." The woman replied in a calm manner. The man's jaw nearly dropped, he had been trying for weeks to figure out what was going on with his coding software, but his efforts were to no avail

"You're serious right?"

"Mhm, see I made this book a while ago, it went from a board game to the software you have now, however it isn't a normal book, the people who have gone into the book I have made voodoo dolls of, I have a whole cupboard full, " the woman chuckled. James just looked at her, this woman was insane, but maybe it was a good idea to try and get more information out of her.

"You don't believe me, do you Spencer?"

The man was a little caught out by the question, and if he had to truthfully answer he would say that he thought she was lying, but again he needed more information.

"No, I believe you" he said sarcastically as he sipped his iced tea.

"Well that's rather good, I'm glad. What would you like to ask Spencer?" The man nearly spat his drink out, this woman could read people ridiculously well.

"Well, when was the the last game"

"Oh well, the game never ends Spencer, so I guess ones happening right now." For the second time that day Spencer's jaw nearly dropped.

"Does that answer your question Spencer." Spencer took a deep breath in and then out.

"Yes that is extremely helpful, in fact it's so helpful, I need to get back to my room to go and sort out the software, thanks Nora."

Spencer got up and started to walk slowly down the hallway. As soon as he was out of Nora's sight he started to speed walk down the hall. As soon as he got to his room he slammed open the door and went straight to his computer. If there were people coming in and out of this game then surely that could be what was messing with the actual coding. At first he didn't want to help them because of his anger, however he thought that he knew all about the game so it could help. He decided that he wanted to help in some way or another, therefore he decided to drop hints into the game so that he could give them an advantage. Dr Spencer James didn't have a way to know if it worked however all he could do was hope.

# Chapter 16

# Growing Suspicion

As everyone walked down the hallways plated with metal boards, the two controllers discover a hint. Trying to avoid suspicion, May diverted the students by discussing how they can escape to get onto the next level.

"So, how are we going to get out?" asked May whilst making eye signals to Pix.

"Do you really think I know?" Ivy snapped at May.

Whilst this conversation took place, Pix removed the cheat code from the corner - at no expense was Pix going to let this experiment fail. It took so long to perfect the experiment. Ivy spotted this and couldn't help but wonder what Pix is doing with the thing she's holding. Ivy asks Ludociel to keep an eye on May and Pix.

Ivy noticed the discrete glances that May delivered towards Pix and thought of it as rather strange. What were they signalling? Were they planning something? There were so many questions but Ivy had but no answers to them. As a result of that, they decided to keep a close eye on them. However throughout the next part of their journey, whenever Ivy would look at Pix and May, they would always be doing something suspicious and secretive. Whether it would be hand gestures or looking at each other constantly. It almost reminded Ivy of two school girls that had a secret to hide.

"How are you getting on?" May interrogated.

"I'm doing as best as I can with the situation, how about you?"

"Ivy's becoming a bit of a problem but the rest are unaware."

"They're going to catch on soon." Pix grew more and more worried and anxious.

"But they haven't yet, so we carry on, ok?" May was staring at Pix with eyes wider than a squirrels

"Yes!" Sighed Pix aggressively. She knew that she needed to walk away while she still had her anger intact. She wanted control over the situation at hand, but that was not going to happen with May there. She knew who wore the trousers well, in this case long black trousers. May always wore black, with hints of white. White to symbolise the owls, because they are the bringer of deaths. Everyone always thought that. Never said but always thought. She had tightly curled hair as black as the night. Even the exorcist wouldn't be able to help her. She had a walk that said I am me. She had a limp sometimes. It was only when she rested too much. Her skin tone was brown and it glistened in the light. However Pix was much different. Her hair brown always messy, she always looked unkempt or unloved. She had no family to care for. No mother to spit on a cloth and wipe the dirt off her face. No father to make sure she's not bullied. No siblings to annoy her. She was lonely. She loved marshmallows. You almost never saw her without a bag of the stuff. There were pieces around her mouth and when she bent down a cracker always fell out of her pocket.

Ivy wandered around contemplating on what to do. Should they reach out to someone else? Did they have enough information to prove their conjectures or was this just the creation of confusion, maybe they were just being oversuspicious. They shook their head. They should just keep finding shiny things instead of sticking their noses in things like this. They thought that the shiny option was the best. They could be wrong after all, but they still had absolutely no reason to trust these two. They haven't really said anything about who they were. They haven't really talked to anyone but Ludociel. They were not even concerned about the people. They didn't know them so why should they, butt into their business?

# Chapter 17

# Where the blame lies

Ivy's gut feeling was telling them that something was wrong about May, every single hint that they get is immediately denied by her, Pix and the teacher. May was the most suspicious, when everyone wasn't looking she slipped in and out of the room. Ivy tried to follow May when she left but the dirty brown haired person always got distracted by shiny objects or anything they saw in the corner of their eye. No matter how strange the objects are they would always pick them up and store them.

May was panicking; she didn't know what to do, the more and more she left the other's the more she could feel that eerie feeling of being watched. She needed to clear herself of any suspicion or the others would be exposed as well. May even though being the cold hearted person she was, she cared for Pix and 'El' if they got caught their year long plans would go straight down the drain. So she made the executive decision to stop meeting 'El' at least until her suspicions were cleared.

Though of course, no one could ever prove that May is involved with anything right? Especially not that weird plant kid known as Ivy. Nobody really knows much about her. She doesn't know how they got suspicious though? Whatever it is, May was going to have to tone down and maybe let Pix take over as Ivy would never suspect one of their friends to be a traitor. Ivy thinks that May being suspicious yet they're the one picking up weird objects.

How could Ivy execute a plan without getting caught out? It would be pretty difficult. They thought about it, pondering their choices. What could they do? They could expose them right here and right now, though that would work, afterall.

"Ooh- is that something shiny? Wait,

what was I talking about again?"

"Oh- right.. My choices." They were brainstorming about it until they thought about their final choice, with many interruptions on the way to their final decision it was finally here. They had finally decided what they were going to do.

Ivy had decided to tell Scarlett of the recent events that they had witnessed, but Ivy was scared in case Scarlett didn't believe them. Should they take the risk or should they let sleeping dogs lie? They all worked up the courage to speak to Scarlett after drawing something in the blood stained walls. They walked over to where Scarlett was, they were about to greet the woman, but they tripped, landing face down. Scarlett ran over to where the strange child was picking them up and putting them on their feet.

"Ivy, are you okay?" Scarlett asked them, her voice was laced with concern.

"Yup, yup oh! Lady, I was just about to ask you something anyways!" Ivy exclaimed.

"Hm? What is it that concerns you?" Scarlett questioned.

Everyone was unaware of the things going on behind the screen. The controllers Pix, May and El' were making sure that no one knew anything about the hints, Nora or Spencer James. The controllers were going to make sure of it. If anyone found out about anything, everything the controllers had worked for would be down the drain completely. They needed to keep that one odd plant child from saying anything to anyone, or else there would be huge trouble. If nothing was done Ivy would definitely say something to start some type of trouble, like they always do.

The others were not suspicious of this so luckily they May and Pix could maybe erase the problem at hand. They would take whatever it takes to keep their secret. Their secret that could destroy lives. End lives. They wanted to minimise the risk of other people finding out that would cause too many problems. They wondered if they found them. Would think they were laughing or talking about them behind their backs.

# Chapter 18

# Arguments

Nora felt a sense of sympathy for those stuck in the game as she saw them almost as her own. Though she felt great resentment towards the children, this was a situation like no other. She loved power. She loved authority. Having children gave her that. But this time felt completely different.

The thought of anything bad happening to them resided with Nora and she had to do something, so she wanted to contact Spencer. She bit back the urge to scream and shout and make the poor man cry. After all, her favorite hobby needed to be left to rest every now and then. Instead she was thinking about being diplomatic, even giving something in return for the favour. She even thought about doing some dreaded babysitting. Why was she a nanny for twenty eight years? We will never know, she was good at her job, nobody doubted her, nobody ever thought about saying no either. They knew the consequences, especially if they also liked voodoo. She knew what could happen but she also knew how much control she had.

She thought about how she would feel

if her children were trapped. As much as she hated them she loved them, she wanted the best for them. All she could think of is what if it was her children in the game. She was filled with guilt. She had to stop it. She wouldn't let harm come to them. She was too moralled. She was filled with pride and doing the right thing. That was partly why she wanted to write the book to show people right from wrong. She wanted to teach them about real life choices and how hard it is to choose sometimes.

She was going to confront him. She was going to be kind but stern and if all else failed her hobby could come to light. Making people cry is her favorite thing. Sadly it didn't work with her husband as making him cry was too much of a task however children, that was a different matter. She walked towards the university campus, she knew the layout of the place better than the back of her own hand. After all, she was a professor. A professor of many subjects but mainly Religious Education and English. Nora's self esteem was already through the roof; she didn't need courage. She came to the door she knocked. There was no reply. She opened the door. He stood there in casual clothes, streetwear to be more precise. She was appalled if her children dare even ask for such clothing they would be praying, religious or not. "I need a favour from you, " she gathered her breath for her next sentence. "It has to stop. I can't do it anymore. These are people in need of assistance. We will help them it is wrong to keep them there. The game will end tonight." She braced herself for an argument. Nora was not one for losing an argument.

"NO. I won't do it. Sorry Nora but no." Spencer screamed.

He realized what he just said.

His face went bright red like a tomato. He knew what was about to happen, he instantly regretted it, It was too late, he had already spoken. He had spoken in a fit of rage, now he had to pay for the consequences. He stepped back and held the table behind him for support. His mind was racing. Nothing anybody could say or do would stop the ending now. He didn't know what was about to happen and with Nora it was unpredictable.

"I beg your pardon, what did you just say to me?" Her intention was to belittle him and make him feel weak. This method

137

never failed with Nora and it wasn't going to fail now. She wanted to curse him there and then. She had a voodoo doll in her pocket. She could do it if she wanted but she wanted to do it right. The correct way. The way her mother had taught her. She sighed and turned around, starting to walk away.

Filled with rage, she stormed home. Her Husband saw her ranting to herself and decided to take cover and take the children for a walk. Making their way swiftly through the back door making sure not to be seen. She burst through the front door unaware she had knocked over her smallest child Bernie who had sadly been left behind in the rush. She charged down the basement stairs like a raging bull. She found parts to a voodoo doll unused and

as frightening as ever. This will be enough
to make the devil turn away, she thought.
She has calmed now knowing justice will
be done, nobody says no to Nora and lives
to tell the tale.

She thought of the most evil curse ever
made. The MOST PAINFUL. THE MOST
HURTFUL. THE ONE THAT'S LIFE CHAN-
GING. However, she resisted the urge. She
made a more practical plan. A plan that
would work and he would be forced. She
chanted words that would make a page
curl up. adly words that should never be
repeated. There was a flash. A BANG.
She felt lighter, more in control. She smiled
to herself softly feeling less angered. She
knew justice will be done. She will, she
has never lost before and she wasn't going
to start now. Her voodoo doll had never

failed her. She trusted it. It had bright red eyes and horns that made her bleed when she touched it. It was large and heavy. It was filled full of children's excrement and as soon as she had cursed the person she would leave the doll outside their home.

# Chapter 19

# Truth revealed

Spencer woke up in a daze. The world was spinning. He felt heavy and fueled with anger. He recognised where he was. He was in his own game. Nora had said the way she got everyone into the book was by making a voodoo doll of them so does that mean that she had made a doll of him and then he ended up in the game.

He couldn't believe she had done this to him. He had trusted her and they were meant to be a team. He didn't hate her, he envied her power. He knew he needed to find the people in the game AS SOON AS POSSIBLE. Slowly but surely he stood up, his legs were wobbly like a newborn deer. He stood for a moment trying to regain his balance and as soon as he did he went off trying to find these people.

"Where could they be, surely they couldn't have gone far." And then he heard it. Then the voices of people came closer, his slow walking became speedy as he followed the voices. As he went around the corner he saw a group of people. They all turned almost simultaneously in his direction.

When he entered the game he had kept his knowledge from the real world and he

wanted to let as many people as he could
know what was going on. As soon as he
saw the people he was looking for, the relief washed over him. Daniel liked Spencer
from the first sight and so Daniel tried
making conversation with him but just as
he opened his mouth to speak May butted
in and said

"Who are you?" She had trust issues
with new people that she didn't know a
lot about. She had acted the same around
all the others but now she was comfortable
around them partly because she didn't want
anyone to suspect Pix of anything and partly
because she had gone through a whole game
with these people and it would look very
bad if she didn't at least try and make conversation with them. Sometimes May had
seen Daniel look over at her and she was

sure that Ashley was jealous every time Daniel tried to make conversation with May! Maybe if Ashley tried to make more friends then she wouldn't need Daniel as much as she does now.

"I am Dr Spencer James and I am the creator of this game. Well me and Nora but that's a long story.I will explain that later."

Daniel looked at May. May saw the look Ashley gave her and she was sure that Daniel nudged Ashley as if to say stop. Everyone else was in silence until the sound of a bottle of coke broke it. Ivy had opened the drink. They didn't read the room and thought that it was a good time. She seemed scared but why? In truth May wasn't scared but she was shocked. She kept thinking, why is the creator here, wouldn't he know

144

about the controllers and who they are? She looked around the room thinking who else she could speak to about her questions. Of course she didn't trust anyone and she really didn't want to speak to anybody but in her need to know the answer to these questions she had to. She needed to get Pix on her own.

"Pix can I speak to you?" May asked.

"Sure."

Pix replied, confused. "What if this Spencer person knows about the controllers and who you actually are?"

She looked at Spencer with worry. "I don't know, I just hope he doesn't."

"Ok, thanks."

Dr Spencer James found a group of people. Eventually he started to ramble however after about ten words. Pix spoke to

Spencer for the first time in a while.

"Sorry to interrupt, but if you haven't noticed we are trying to escape this death game and we have practically no time to lose."

Spencer stopped for a minute as he looked at the girl. He really thought she was rude, he was simply trying to help yet this girl was trying to stop him.

"And who are you?" Spencer said in a rather frustrated tone.

"The name's Pix, but does that really matter right now?"

"Could you just stop bickering and let the man speak?" another young woman spoke up. May looked at Pix and Pix looked back at May.

"He can speak later, we need to go now." Pix grabbed May and Scarlett's arms and everyone else followed. As they were all leaving, May grabbed Spencer's arm.

May dragged Spencer over to the corner. "Hey why'd you do that? Stop. I was trying to do something?!"

"I'm sorry but you were saying too much, " May said with a cold tone.

"And because of that you'll have to disappear temporarily.You're lucky. " May grabbed Spencer's warm hand with her cold one and began to drag him away. Slipping out of the room unnoticed by the others except for one, Ivy. They saw everything. May lead Spencer down a labyrinth of corridors, to a cloaked figure. May kneeled down on one knee and spoke

"El I have brought him. The one who's been trying to help them escape." The end of May's sentence sounded like a snarl.

"Thank you."

El' reached out their hand and touched Spencer. In a flash they both began to glitch away leaving just May there. May walked back with a feeling of dread and satisfaction. She slipped back into the room unnoticed and joined the crowd. A small sense of relief washed over her. May couldn't believe that she had got rid of Spencer! She was happy until she walked back into the room and heard everyone say

"Where is Spencer?"

"He is not here and he won't be coming back!" Daniel, who really liked May, stood forward and said

"What have you done with him, May?"

# Chapter 20

# Trauma Revisited

After May came back, the group continued and found another challenge they had to complete. This time they had to relive something that happened in the past.The group didn't know this but this was going to be very personal and something the group probably wouldn't enjoy.

Daniel was first to relive his past. He sat watching his ten year old memory run through his head and the scene of his parents leaving the house and trying to stop them as they finished packing their bags into the car. He could hear his child's voice shouting: "MUM DAD DON'T GO PLEASE!!" When his mum and dad were talking to his babysitter he snuck into the car. The car drove all the way to the M6 and it was raining very heavily. His Mum called Daniel and he had to say something back because they knew he was there.

"Daniel come here." He went over and sat on her lap.

"What is that idiot doing?" shouted his dad. His mum looked really scared and she told his dad to pull over. When he pulled over she told Daniel to get out of the car and when he did she shut the door and his dad drove off. He saw his mum poke her head out of the window and mouth, "Sorry." The truck was swerving everywhere and Daniel's dad didn't like it so he tried to drive past it but as soon as he was level with the truck, it swerved and Daniel's dad swerved to get out of the way and all Daniel saw was the car flip and fly off the edge of a cliff. When he saw this happen he felt his heart break, like he'd never be happy ever again. He went to the end of the cliff and saw the car at the bottom. He was a good climber and he climbed down to the bottom of the cliff and saw that his parents were holding hands and they had a smile on their face. He knew he would never be able to forget the memory and so he ran away from there. He kept going and didn't look back. Then he ran away from home all because his parents died. He kept thinking it was his fault that they were dead. He found a cave and lived in it, however he still had to travel to school so he had to wake up extra early in the mornings. The memory ended and he kept remembering how hard it was for him without a mum and dad.

"You have been traumatized yet you are still happy. Why??" Daniel knew why he had always been happy and whenever he told people why he was still positive about life it always made people well up with tears.

"Because my mum and dad wouldn't want me to be upset about them. They would want me to live on and get a good job."

The voice replied by saying

"I bet they are disappointed though because you haven't got a job have you?"

"NO, no they've always said that no matter what I did they would always be proud of me. I haven't got a job but I am trying and I want to achieve the best for my life and if I ever get a family of my own then I will do my best to make them proud."

"You should not be so positive about a negative thing!"

"But if I am so negative about traumatic stuff then how can I get on with life?"

"Why can't you be like May? All negative about life!"

"Because you can't live properly if you have negative thoughts!" When saying this he was thinking about his mum and dad. He found a crowbar and smashed the mirror. Behind the mirror was a door and he walked through it very casually, head held high thinking, hoping if he had made his Mum and Dad proud.

Pix came from a normal family. She always got good grades and she mainly kept herself to herself. Until one day, a day that would change her life forever. No one knows who or why, a group of people burned down her house, until the house that's wall were full of memories were burned to the ground. Pix was the only survivor, however that is not where this story ends. The group of people realized that Pix was alive, what do you do with a child who could snitch on you, you ask, well you take it. At least that's what these people thought.

They planned to torture her and then just simply hide the body. However that is not how it worked out. After being there for a while she would look down and see scars, scars of a knife and scars of when she got burnt. She was bruised and clearly was in pain, long ago. She was traumatised. Everytime she even looks down she will remember. Pix had obviously had enough. So when it was dark and the people were drunk and knocked out. She ran and she started a life for herself. She never attended school and instead played games and tried to live in her own fantasy world. That opportunity came along when she started to play a new game. At that time someone starts to speak to her and eventually convinces her to join. That person being Elextha otherwise known as El'.

Her memories flash as the scene of her dad burning keeps appearing as she runs off because she was scared of what would actually happen if she stayed. She watched herself run off crying in the traumatizing memory.

Ashley's memory of her sitting with Daniel shows as she watches herself talking to him "Hey Danny I have something to tell you" Daniel looks at her smiling. She loved his smile as she panicked and she couldn't confess. "You're gonna lose this game!" she smiles pretending and trying not to cry as she really couldn't tell him and the memory slowly fades.

Ivy watches their friends go into a zone out mode as they looked at their friends confused playing around in the grass waiting patiently for their friends.

They all came back to their normal state and began thinking about what had just happened. They were all slightly confused but all decided to not speak a word and move on because these moments to them were their biggest secrets and they wouldn't tell anyone.

# Chapter 21

# Secrets Revealed

After the group had experienced their past again and they were back together they walked quietly into a blank white room completely oblivious to their surroundings. Some sort of spirit type creature started making its way towards the group, humming a tune leaving them all stunned as to what they were witnessing. The creature was a tall figure covered in a black dress with a veil covering the face of said creature.

The spirit type creature slowly made its way towards the group and pulls up the veil. Underneath the vail is a face no one ever thought they would see again.

"Elextha-"

is all that is heard, until Pix speaks up

"You died, I saw you with my own eyes. How are you here! Are you really Elextha, anyways?"

Elextha stayed silent and chuckled. The way his voice sounded led them to believe that something had changed within Elextha. There was a pause before he spoke again.

"You all have to reveal one big truth about yourself or your life. If you don't ad-

mit something you do not get to go through
and will get killed."

Elextha's voice sounded like he was trying not to laugh. No one found it amusing
though. The group began to panic about
the secret they had to share with Elextha.

Ashley decided it was best for her to
reveal her secret first and Daniel decided
he would go after her. Ashley began,

"Well-l my deepest-t secret is.."

Ashley paused, her cheeks now flushed.

"I-I love DANIEL!"

The last part was blurted out so fast
Daniel didn't have time to react before
Elextha spoke again

"That is correct, next person may go."

Everyone looked over to where Daniel
was, he now stood his mouth wide open
and his cheeks a bright red.

"Uh-h mm-y secret-t is that- I l-love Ashley–" It was Ashleys turn to be surprised. After they had both got over the initial shock.

"Elextha, is that correct?" Pix asked in a dark tone.

"Indeed it is."

Ashley and Daniel were now embraced in a hug crying tears of joy. May spoke next, her voice was flat with no emotion,

"My secret is that I sacrificed my parents to the devil. For pure revenge. I still don't regret what I did." Everyone gasped, no one expected those words to come out of May. She was a mole but no one expected her to be heartless. All Elextha did was nod in agreement not wanting to speak much more than needed. Next the plant kid spoke, the plant kid was a nickname for Ivy.

"My secret issssss- once Bartholomew Baguette the First, jumped from a cliff, with a broken wingy, I dropped a piano on him!"

"He was a bird. They loved him more than anything or so we thought."

Elextha chuckles and agrees. The teacher spoke next, her voice sounding more like a sob.

"I-I accidentally killed my dad with witchcraft, I still regret it to this day." Scarlett instantly regretted admitting this.

"I never meant to." She started sobbing.

Everyone felt sympathy towards the teacher, unlike May who did it purposely Scarlett didn't mean to, meanwhile Scarlett has begun to cry her eyes began to swell and puff up. The only person left was Pix. Pix didn't want to speak in front of the traitor. She clamped her mouth shut and stood there and challenged Elextha.

"You absolute idiot, " Pix said through gritted teeth.

"I really thought you died, you know."

"Hm?" Elextha chuckled darkly,

"You should know me better Pix, considering you are one of us."

Before any of the other people in the room could blink. Pix ran up to Elextha and stabbed him in the face. The pocket knife stabbed elextha's eye and they both struggled until, Pix won. Elextha now blinded, he grabbed where his eye was clearly in a lot of pain, and fell to the ground.

"Not so smug now are we El'?" Elextha let out a grunt in response, clearly not wanting to waste his energy. He pulled his now blood soaked hand away from it, his eyes now shut. Elextha shakely stood up, and tried to grab Pix only to be met with a stab to the hand.

"Stop resisting- let me kill you." Pix snarled as she knocked him to the ground. The more weight Pix put onto Elextha's arm, the more you could hear the crunch of what sounded like a bone. Elextha grew desperate as he clawed at Pix's leg but to no avail. Everyone was in shock; they couldn't believe the scene that was set out in front of them. They wanted to help but the aura coming from the both of them told the others that they wanted to be left alone. Meanwhile, Pix was growing impatient, why wasn't he fighting back she thought, she grabbed the knife tightly and slashed shallow lines into Elextha's chest. Blood spewed out of his mouth, he was now coughing a lot, his breath becoming hoarse. The final blow was delivered as the knife stabbed his heart. Elextha's blood formed a large puddle underneath his body.

After Elextha's body stopped moving, they all looked at each other in horror at the scene that just unfolded in front of them as the door didn't appear, but Pix suddenly removed the pocket knife. After a while of searching the corpse of elextha, Pix removes a book, and as the book is removed a door appears and they walk up to it seeing nothing but black.

"Should we go into it?" Scarlett asked. No one had time to reply.

All of a sudden the group sees a bright light and are pulled into the door one by one. Finally when the last person is pulled through, the door closes behind them creating a loud bang. In the room now was just Elextha's corpse that seemed to no longer be real itself as it started to glitch uncontrollably, until finally it disappeared completely. Was he really dead?

# Chapter 22

# Morals

Each person woke up in a completely different place. The first person to wake up was Daniel. He was in a desolate desert. After Daniel it was Ivy who randomly woke up in a cardboard box in the center of a lake.

Scarlett woke up in her lakeside home seeing her dad confused not knowing what's happening. She slowly realizes what's going on and tears form in her eyes, not being able to move as the scene starts playing and two choices appear as she reads.

"You rather save your dad or you go back to your friends and relive this moment of you- NO I can't choose!" She panics looking at the timer as the scene plays and she starts crying and quickly without looking she chose to live her life and join her friends again. As she relives this moment she cries in pain seeing her dad die in front of her eyes. As she sees the door to get out appear and starts running, crying.

Ashley woke up seeing Daniel and her sitting in her room playing games, as she looked confused not being able to move in any way; slowly looking around realising what's happening to her and as tears form in her eyes she sees her options appear in front of her as she looks at them not knowing what to do. As quickly as she possibly can, choosing not to confess seeing the door appear and running quickly to it as she thinks about what just happened.

Daniel wakes up and sees his parents in his home wondering what's happening tearing up with just seeing his parents as his two choices appear he starts crying softly looking at them and looks at his parents breathing in and out quickly.

"I want you guys to live." he says in a shaky voice and picks the option to try and save his parents as he tells them to stay back and tries to keep them from going which eventually works as he sits with them, he suddenly sees the door running away as his parents disappear.

May wakes up in her home seeing her parents, very quickly realising what's happening trying to keep her emotions in and looking at her two options. She breaks down softly picking the option to save her parents as they start disappearing, her door appears as she runs to it trying to calm herself.

Pix wakes up seeing the fire, the one that killed her parents. Then she felt it, the fear. She dropped to her knees, and then everything became blurred and she fell back. Then she flung herself up, only to realize there was no one there. She looked around for a second and then realized she knew exactly where she was. It was her childhood home. Was she dreaming? No, she was definitely awake. She looked at the door ahead of her. On it

was a huge decorated sign, it had tons of
stickers. A lot of them were from when she
was a kid and she would go to the den-
tist, they would always give her stickers
as a good job. So she would put them on
the door. Some were from when Christ-
mas came around. Everyone knew how
much she loved stickers, so they would give
her stickers, they also gave her those little rubs that looked like objects, she really
loved the animal ones but she would always take them apart and then the pieces
would get lost. She put her fingers against
the door and ran down it, it was odd to
be here again. When she would get bored
he would run her fingernails against the
door, this obviously scratched the wood
off. She backed away and then reached for
the door handle.She twisted it, only to be

met with a hallway. She stepped out and the door slammed behind her, She took a couple steps forward and then heard a familiar crackling noise. She watched as the door to her childhood room went up in flames. She turned around, and then scrunched her face up to stop tears flowing down her face. She took a deep breath and then went to keep walking down the same hallway everyone else had walked down.

Ivy woke up in a room not knowing what's happened to them and why no one else is with them, just sat there looking clueless. After a while they realized where they were, they were in the lake from earlier. There seemed to be not a lot around, but then they saw a stick and then they actually met a Glow Squid named Ludociel. He was a very fancy man and no one could

J

disagree, as it is the truth. After searching for a while, Ivy found a plug that drained the river water. After that they found the door that could get them out of the room

Everyone goes through each of their doors and they see each other not knowing what's happening or why everything that's just happened has happened. Daniel and Ashley start speaking to each other and telling each other about their feelings, Scarlett sits there alone contemplating if she made the right decision. Ivy sat next to Scarlett trying to comfort her as Ivy themselves contemplated things. Pix is clueless standing around looking at them all with May. After what seemed like an eternity, something happened. It's not nice though everyone immediately feels like they're drowning in a pit of despair. The group passed

out after a while because of the suffocating
feeling.

# Chapter 23

# Reality?

All of them woke up in a daze. They felt like they had been in a fire and cold water was thrown at them. Everyone looked around. Daniel shot Ashley a loving look. She looked away. She was afraid that if she looked at him she would never look away but instantly, she looked away. She loved him dearly, and all she wanted was to make him happy, however she was afraid that if he was with her, he wouldn't be happy. Ivy pointed and felt everything as they got their bearings. May and Elextha went still, almost like stuffed animals. They all stood up, with the world still spinning.

"Take a seat, Dr Spencer will be here soon." She hated the fact they didn't even sanitize their hands before entering. Nora struggled to get herself back up from the floor, so she decided to lie down and have a nap before they came. She very rarely had sleep because the children kept her up (Sleep deprivation was normal for her.) Nobody said a word. They were still a bit dazed. By the look on Noras face they didn't dare. Spencer burst through the door nearly knocking Nora off her feet.

"Be careful, or do you want to go back

to where you came from? Memories don't fade Spencer, they just get pushed back." She snapped.

She shot him a look of disgust. His feet suddenly became very interesting. Her face dropped. Serious Nora was now present. "I need to talk to you all, It's a sensitive subject."

"It was an experiment." Nora rather abruptly said as they all huddled around. They all sat in a cold lab room. She had never been one for kindness. Kindness only came to people who deserved it. In her mind Ashley should have told Daniel sooner. Love only comes to people who speak up. If she didn't speak up she wouldn't get love and affection. She could see that they were close. Nora and her husband were very close; nobody knew her better than him,

Philip Lynn. That was mostly why she didn't like her mother, her mother didn't know her. Her mother didn't approve of marrying so young, but she chose love and in her mind Ashley and Daniel should have done the same. She viewed them as cowardly and Costa lovers. Nora was a big believer in love at first sight and love chooses you not the other way around. Ivy and May were viewed as weak and in Nora's eyes, that was not a person she wanted to know. Nora was raised old fashioned. The women should raise their children. Women should be feared. The women should always be in control. It was a wartime thing. Women finally had power. In her mind it was about time. Her husband liked it that way, as did she. Scarlett asked, "What do you mean?"

"Well, we wanted to see how you would react under certain situations. We wanted to see if you were moral and full of pride and a good person for this earth." She gathered her breath to continue and to see how they would react.

"Some of you have passed. Personally, I wouldn't have done the same; still, I hope you rethink your life now with Ashley."

"Elextha, I am very disappointed, not only with you but with all of your decisions!"

Ashley shot her a look, she quickly turned away when she realised she was right. Life is short. She should savour the moment until it's a memory.

"You can all go home now." Nora said. "It was all a game; to be honest, the less you know the better."

"W-w-w-what do you mean we can all just go home?   After all that has happened, you honestly expect us to be fine and go home?"   whispered Ashley under her breath.

# Chapter 24

# The Spork

Spencer was in shock from everything that he had witnessed. Instead of informing them of all that had happened, he decided to keep himself muted as it was all too much to process. They all decided they should leave as they were all so confused as to what they had just experienced. It had all begun when they had just planned to have a party and have fun, but they ended up taking part in an experiment that left them all stunned. Even though they all agreed to join this experiment, they had all completely forgotten about it, until they were awoken by two strangers who they now know as Nora and Dr Spencer, they were never aware that it was an experiment, it was all so realistic. It was an eye opening experience for them all.

"Guys, let's go back to my house, and let's never play a video game again." Ashley said to the group. The whole group was quiet as they walked back. What do you do in this situation, a lot of them were completely traumatized. They didn't know left from right, they were terrified that it would happen again. They could do nothing to stop it if it did happen. The group were completely overthinking everything after they had left.

"I feel sick and dizzy, my head doesn't feel attached to me."

They all entered Ashley's house in a completely quiet manner. They all just stood, they were traumatized from what they had been through. I mean after all, the whole Elextha thing and seeing the things that messed them up in the first place.

"So erm, I'll never play any games after this!" Daniel chuckled. He was trying to lighten the mood and it was working but barely. Ashley let out a small laugh, knowing that he was completely lying.

"Anyone remember anything about what happened before?" Daniel spoke again.

"Well I remember seeing you and Ashley cuddling on the couch." May said while holding back a laugh. Daniel's face went a shade of red.

"I meant something useful." Then a voice spoke up,

"LOOK, my spork!" Ivy screamed in delight.

"How do you have that Ivy?" Ashley asked, surprised. They all looked at each other with a confused expression on their faces.

"Why would you have a spork?" May asked suspiciously.

"I don't know, it must be from the experiment."

They all concluded that the spork must have derived from the experiment - but how come Dr Spencer forgot about it? How did this all happen? How did they go from

186

being at a party to being in some unnatural universe? One could only speculate what sorcery must have generated such an intelligent creation. Maybe it wasn't an experiment. No, no way! They woke up and they saw Nora and Doctor Spencer. There is nothing that suggests that this isn't an experiment. Plus nothing like that stupid game room thing is real. How silly to even suggest anything other than that.

Ashley let out a small sigh,

"Maybe we should go for a small walk to clear our minds!" The whole group completely agreed and decided to go with her. They walked around for a bit. Everything just seemed to go slowly, everyone was really trying to figure out whether this whole thing was real or not. I mean like they said before there was no way this whole thing was real. Ashley walked forward and stopped at the edge of the pavement to make sure there were no cars coming. She walked out in the road and then heard an incredibly loud noise coming from her right. That's when she saw a bus coming her way. She completely froze, then she heard Daniel scream out her name. She was waiting for the impact to hit her body. But it didn't, it never did.

*The world is a tree and we are all dead. The earth is fake, nothing is real  Ludociel*
*THE END*

# Our Authors

## Scarlet Best

My name is Scarlet Best and I loved making this book. I love English so I was proud to make this book and I made it with my friends. I love how we had an idea and we agreed on everything people said. I enjoyed making up characters. My characters are Lucifer and Daniel. Writing about them and seeing them come to life was just an amazing experience. My favorite part was probably when we put the whole book together and when we helped each other out. One more thing: I would like to thank all my English teachers that I have had in the past for helping me get better at English. Mr Barlow also arranged for us to do this so a massive thank you to him! YwY

## Evie Davidson

I'm Evie and I believe that this could be a
strange version of Scooby Doo and the Cyberchase. I also watched Cyberchase while
writing. :0) This is a happy man. This is a
sad man :0( . They are roommates. That
is all I have to say. VuV

## Melanie Jones

My name is MeIanie Jones. I loved making this book. We all had a laugh about Costa lovers and it has been a great week. I hope you enjoyed the book, as we have all worked so extremely hard on it. My character was Nora Lynn. I made her as she seemed relatable and the sort of person who everyone turned to for support. She was a character I very much liked. My mum loves Victorian clothes so I thought I might include that. Every little thing I could think of I included as Nora Lynn. With the seventeen children I asked my friend to pick a number so that's the number we had. We did this book in one week. I loved seeing them coming together and coming to life. Mr Barlow was a massive help with this book and has always been

a great support. However I don't think he
would agree with Nora about Costa. OxO

## Lauren Hill

My name is Lauren and I liked doing this as it was fun to make a character and their backstory and eventually seeing them come to life in the story with all of the other characters that we created together. I created Ashley because I think she is someone who we can all relate to. I found this very fun to do and I enjoyed it. Thanks Mr Barlow. And you're watching Disney channel!! VnV

## Sandra Korejwo

My name is Sandra and I am 14 Years Old. I loved doing this for the week especially because I missed lessons. Joking for legal reasons. But really this week was a lot of fun and I honestly had the best time. Now about myself: I love art and cooking and most importantly I LOVE kpop. I hope that from this experience I can really learn in the future even though I don't want to do English in the future but anyways I am happy I got to experience this. In case you were wondering, my favourite cheese is mimolette melty cheese. QwQ

## Kiana Onyiriuka

My name is Kiana and I am 14 years old. YnY My favourite subjects are PE and Foriegn Languages. In my spare time I like to play sports and video games. I also love to watch TV shows and listen to music. I based my character (Dr Spencer James) on many things. My character's hobbies are based on a few of mine. I am really proud of my character as it didn't take long to make but is really in depth. I enjoyed this experience as it was an outlet for my creativity and just overall fun.

## Poppy Phillips

My name is Poppy - I'm 13? 14? TvT
Who really knows - I like to draw! :¿ And
I prefer to draw digitally rather - than tra-
ditionally! My character Elextha is uh -
made up - totally - so I got to murder them
off - and most gore may or may not - be
written by mwah. Uh - I play Zelda and I
like to listen to music a lot ig - i like to talk
to people online but never irl - so yeah -
there's all about me ig - UwU

## Emily Saidi

My name is Emily and I'm 14 going on 15. I love school and my favourite subject is Science. I have enjoyed writing this book with my peers as it's a way to collectively join ideas and work as a team. The character that I formed was May. In a way, I relate with her as we're both introverted and keep ourselves to ourselves, however I have added significant contrast within our personalities. I love watching anime (my favourite is The Seven Deadly Sins), sci-fi and action movies. For the future, I have many aspirations which is why I work hard, as I have the need to be successful! I listen to a wide selection of music such as - Drill, Hip Hop, RnB and Indie. But overall, I like to have a good time and make people laugh! QxQ

P.S. I'd like to thank my English teacher Mr B for creating this amazing opportunity.

## Ella Twadell

Hi my name is Ella, I wrote the character Pix. I based a lot of her personality on myself and the things I like. This was a really cool experience, and I really enjoyed all of it. I enjoyed doing this with both my best friends. I really enjoyed writing about my character. Oh also hi to my family, friends, classmates and teachers reading this, I hope you really enjoyed it. Also thanks to my dog, she kinda inspired Pix's lazy attitude. :0)

Printed in Great Britain
by Amazon

83247951R00120